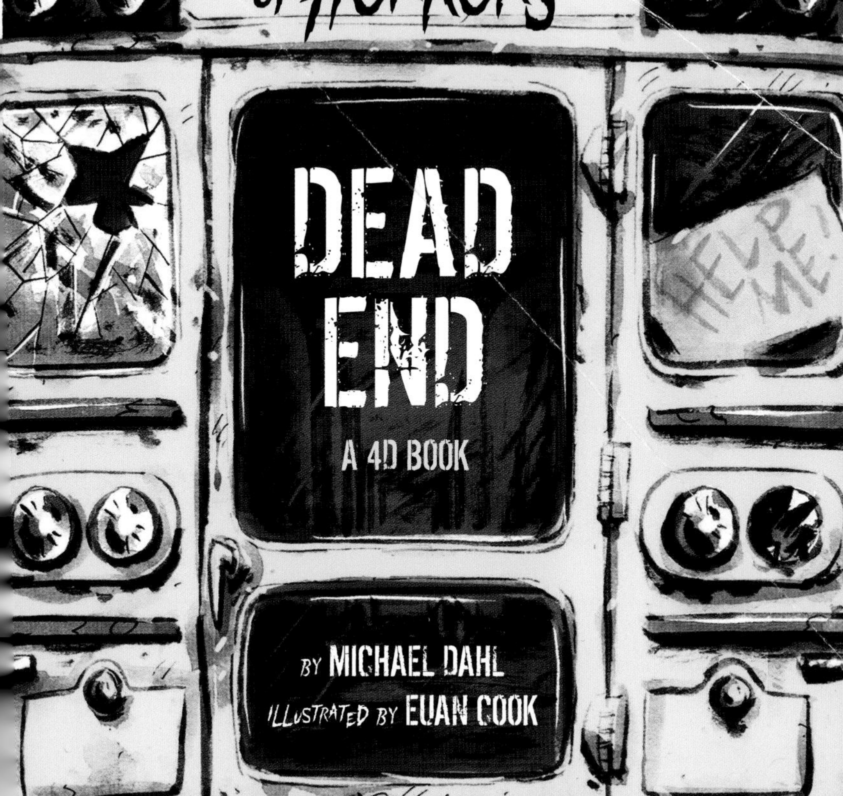

STONE ARCH BOOKS
a capstone imprint

School Bus of Horrors is published by
Stone Arch Books
A Capstone Imprint
1710 Roe Crest Drive
North Mankato, Minnesota 56003
www.mycapstone.com

Cataloging-in-Publication Data is available at the Library of Congress website.
ISBN 978-1-4965-6268-5 (library binding)
ISBN 978-1-4965-6274-6 (paperback)
ISBN 978-1-4965-6280-7 (eBook PDF)

Summary: After detention, a young boy steps aboard the late bus. When the bus takes an unexpected turn toward a graveyard, his long day suddenly goes from bad to worse.

Designer: Bob Lentz
Production Specialist: Tori Abraham

Cover background by Shutterstock/oldmonk

Printed in the United States of America.
PA021

Download the Capstone  app!

- Ask an adult to download the Capstone 4D app.
- Scan the cover and stars inside the book for additional content.

When you scan a spread, you'll find fun extra stuff to go with this book! You can also find these things on the web at www.capstone4D.com using the password: dead.62685

TABLE OF CONTENTS

From dawn to dusk, the **SCHOOL BUS OF HORRORS** rumbles along city streets and down country roads, searching for another passenger. Yellow, black markings, dirty windows—it looks like any other.

But **BEWARE!** Step aboard this bus and

experience the scariest ride of your life . . .

CHAPTER ONE

DEAD MEAT

Braden sits on the afternoon school bus.

He stares at a paper in his hand.

Braden does not want to go home.

At the top of the paper is a large F.

When Mom and Dad find out I failed, Braden thinks, *I am dead meat!*

Braden glances around the bus.

It looks different than the bus that usually drives him home.

The windows are dirty. The floor is covered in mud.

The driver can't be seen. He sits behind a safety wall of thick plastic.

Braden is the last passenger.

The street corner by his house is always the final stop.

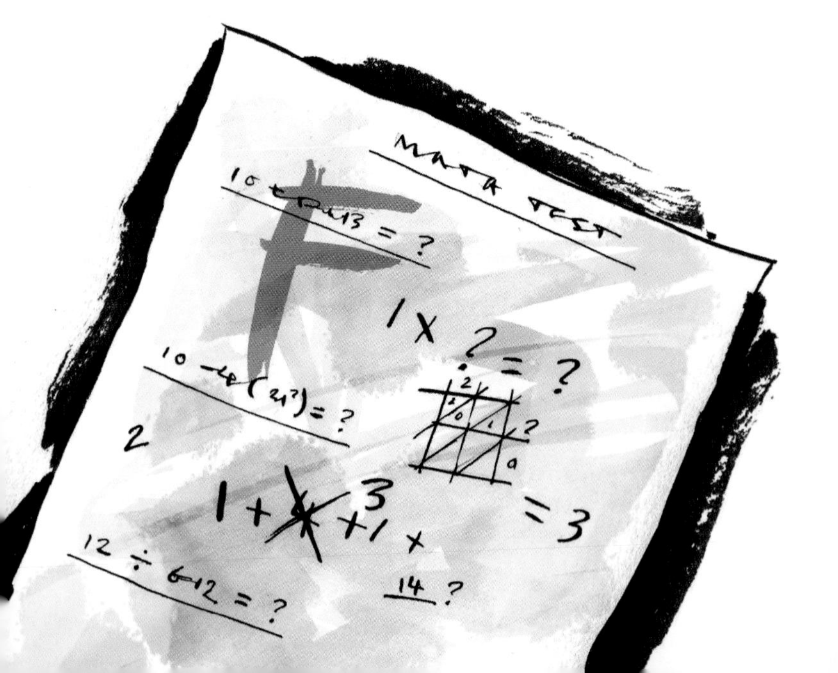

"I can't show this test to my parents," he whispers to himself. "Maybe I'll run away."

Then Braden sniffs.

Smells like rotten meat in here, he thinks.

Braden is surprised to feel the bus slowing down.

He leans over to the window.

He wipes away some of the grime with his hand.

The sun has already set.

It is hard to see through the smudged glass.

But Braden sees shadows moving toward the bus.

The road is filled with an endless crowd of people.

CHAPTER TWO
NO ONE SPEAKS

Hundreds and hundreds of people stream past the bus.

Why are they all moving in the same direction? Braden wonders.

The driver stops the bus.

Suddenly, with a whoosh of air, the door opens.

Braden gets up and walks to the front of the bus.

He stares at the open door.

Then he turns to look back at the plastic wall around the driver.

"Did you open the door?" asks Braden.

The driver does not answer.

Braden slowly climbs down the steps and onto the road.

"What's going on?" he asks the crowd.

No one speaks.

Braden looks down at the road.

And why isn't anyone wearing shoes? he wonders.

Braden follows the crowd across the road and down a small slope.

Up ahead is a large wall with a gate.

Above the gate hangs a sign made of curving metal bars: CENTRAL CEMETERY.

CENTRAL CEMETERY

CHAPTER THREE

THE GRAVE

A crush of people surround Braden.

He tries to get away, but there are too many bodies.

He yells and shouts, but no one pays any attention to him.

The crowd pushes and bumps him along.

Suddenly, the crowd stops moving.

He steps forward into a small clearing.

The silent strangers are standing next to a newly dug grave.

It smells like rotting meat.

Braden steps closer to the open grave.

He looks carefully at the stone above the hole.

The dead person's name is in shadow. But Braden can read a date on the stone.

The date is *his* birthday!

Braden feels a sudden chill.

He tries to step away from the grave.

The crowd is closing in on him. Their hands reach out to him.

Braden shouts!

He falls into the open hole.

CHAPTER FOUR
THE LAST STOP

SQUUUUUUUEEEEEEEEK!

Braden blinks his eyes.

He is sitting on the school bus once more.

The bus stops with a squeal of brakes.

The door opens.

Braden rushes to the front of the bus.

He peers out the door and sees a dark street corner.

It is his stop. The last stop.

He sees his house sitting back from the street.

Braden leaps out of the bus.

As soon as his feet hit the sidewalk, he takes a deep breath.

The test paper is crumpled in his hand.

He doesn't care about the F anymore.

He cannot wait to be home.

SCHOOL BUS

GLOSSARY

CEMETERY (SEM-uh-ter-ee)—a place where dead people are buried

GLANCE (GLANSS)—to look at something very quickly

GRIME (GRIME)—dirt or soot that has built up on a surface

PASSENGER (PASS-uhn-jur)—someone other than the driver who travels in a vehicle

ROTTEN (ROT-uhn)—something that has gone bad or started to smell and decay

SMUDGED (SMUHGD)—made a messy mark by rubbing something

DISCUSS

1. Why do you believe the author titled this book *Dead End*?

2. At the beginning of the story, Braden is afraid to go home. At the end, he is happy to finally be at his house. Why do you think his mood changed?

3. What lesson do you think Braden learned from riding the School Bus of Horrors?

WRITE

1. Create a new title for this book. Then write a paragraph on why you chose your new title.

2. Write another ending for this book. Maybe Braden doesn't make it home. Maybe he must jump off the moving bus! You decide.

3. Write about the scariest bus ride you've ever experienced.